Cat Baby

by Pat Thomson

illustrated by Dee Shulman

PICTURE WINDOW BOOKS
Minneapolis, Minnesota

Editor: Nick Healy
Page Production: Melissa Kes
Art Director: Nathan Gassman
Associate Managing Editor: Christianne Jones

First American edition published in 2007 by
Picture Window Books
5115 Excelsior Boulevard
Suite 232
Minneapolis, MN 55416
877-845-8392
www.picturewindowbooks.com

This Americanization of CAT BABY was originally published in English in
2003 under the title MARY-ANNE AND THE CAT BABY by arrangement
with Oxford University Press.

Printed in the United States of America.

Library of Congress Cataloging-in-Publication Data
Thomson, Pat, 1939-
Cat baby / by Pat Thomson ; illustrated by Dee Shulman.
p. cm. — (Read-it! chapter books)
Summary: When she decides to dress her kitten, Muffin, in baby
clothes and stroll around town with her in the carriage, Mary-Anne and
her friend Josh have some unusual mishaps and varied reactions
from friends and neighbors.
ISBN-13: 978-1-4048-3123-0 (library binding)
ISBN-10: 1-4048-3123-1 (library binding)
[1. Cats—Fiction. 2. Animals—Infancy—Fiction. 3. Friendship
—Fiction.] I. Shulman, Dee, ill. II. Title.
PZ7.T3765Cat 2006
[Fic]—dc22   2006027253

Table of Contents

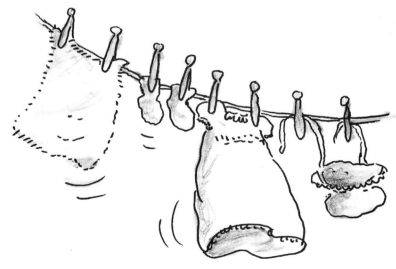

Chapter One

Does your grandmother tell you that children were always good when she was young? Maybe they were, but maybe not. That's all I'm saying.

This happened a long time ago when my grandmother was young.

I'm going to tell you a story about a girl named Mary-Anne.

She was a lively kind of girl. On
Sundays, she could look like a little
angel. She wore colored ribbons in
her long, dark hair.

On other days, she ditched her
ribbons, and her hair stood on end.

She wasn't an only child. She had
three big brothers, one big sister, and
two little sisters.

Oh! I nearly forgot the new baby.

So that was eight children. No wonder their mother was always busy. This meant Mary-Anne often did things without asking for her mother's permission.

If you promise not to copy her, I will tell you about the time Mary-Anne got the cat mixed up with the new baby.

The baby was very small. It slept a lot. It screamed a lot, too. To tell the truth, it was often quite smelly. Mary-Anne didn't like it much.

She also had
a cat. The cat was
quite small, too.
Like the baby, it
slept a lot. But it
never screamed,
and it was cute
and furry.

So sweet!

Oh, yuck!

Mary-Anne
thought Muffin the
cat was much nicer
than the baby.

One morning, only Mary-Anne and her mother were at home. Mother was upstairs with the baby.

Mary-Anne was supposed to peel the potatoes for dinner, but the sun was shining. It looked so nice outside. Perhaps she could go into the yard first, Mary-Anne thought. Just for a minute.

The big carriage was in the yard. Baby carriages in those days were like the carriages horses pulled. They stood high and had bouncy springs.

Mary-Anne touched the carriage.
It bounced. She released the brake
and pushed the handle a little.

Soon, she was parading up and
down the yard, pushing the carriage.

As she passed the gate for the third
time, she heard a shuffling noise
from outside the fence. An eye was
looking at her through a knothole.

I know it's
you, Josh Pembroke!
You might as well
come in!

The latch lifted, and a boy came in. He wasn't like Mary-Anne. He was very neat and clean.

"You're not allowed to touch the carriage," he said.

"It's supposed to be your tongue, silly," said Josh. "Can I give a push?"

Mary-Anne let him. After all, whatever it looked like, Josh was her best friend.

Josh took a turn with the carriage. It was boring, pushing around an empty carriage.

"We need a baby," said Josh.

"Not ours," said Mary-Anne.

The baby's clothes were dancing on the clothesline.

Mary-Anne looked at Muffin. Then she looked at the little bonnet and lacy shawl.

Josh looked, too.

"I'll tell," he said, but he moved out of the way so Mary-Anne could reach the bonnet and shawl.

Mary-Anne wrapped Muffin in the shawl and laid him in the carriage. Then she put on the bonnet and tied it carefully under his chin.

Muffin closed his eyes.

Mary-Anne and Josh looked at each other.

"Open the gate," said Mary-Anne. "Muffin needs to go for a stroll. It's good for him. All babies need to be walked. Mother said so."

And they pushed the carriage out into the street.

Chapter Two

Mary-Anne and Josh paraded
down Main Street, pretending to
be grown-ups. They stopped and
looked in the shop windows.

"Where shall we go?" asked Josh.

"Well," said Mary-Anne, "my
mother always goes past the butcher
shop, past the grocery store, and into
the candy shop."

"She does not!" replied Josh. "She goes into all of the other shops."

They waved to the grocer. He came out of his shop and stood by the fruit and vegetables.

"Doing the shopping?" he asked.

"Yes," said Mary-Anne, "and walking the baby."

"Good of you to help your mom," added Mr. Green, nodding. He smiled at someone behind them.

Then Mr. Green said, "Good morning, Mr. Burton."

Mary-Anne and Josh looked at each other.

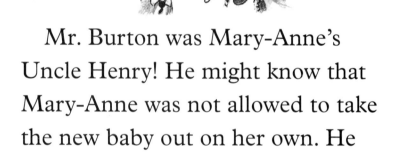

Mr. Burton was Mary-Anne's Uncle Henry! He might know that Mary-Anne was not allowed to take the new baby out on her own. He might look in the carriage.

Mr. Green came over to them and put his hand on the carriage handle.

"Here are two good children," he said. "Your niece is helping her mom look after the new baby."

"Is she now!" said Uncle Henry.

Both men bent over and looked into the carriage.

"What the … ?" gasped Mr. Green.

"Mary-Anne!" said Uncle Henry. "What are you up to?"

Both men started to laugh.

"Your new nephew will have to start shaving soon," said Mr. Green. "Look at those whiskers!"

"Good head of hair, too," said Uncle Henry. "Takes after me."

They laughed again, and Uncle Henry gave the kids a penny each.

"Thank you, Uncle Henry," said Mary-Anne in a small, polite voice.

Mr. Green picked out two apples and rubbed them on his apron.

"Here you are, kids," he said.

"Thanks, Mr. Green," they said.

They looked at each other. Then they both looked at the candy shop.

They parked the carriage and stood gazing in the window.

Candy did not come in wrappers back then. It was in big glass jars. The kids took a long time to choose.

Finally, Josh chose the caramels, and Mrs. Munns poured out a penny's worth into a little cone of paper. Mary-Anne chose a big stick of rock candy.

As they left, Josh tripped over the step and nearly choked on his caramel. Mary-Anne had to give him a big thump on his back.

They strolled away down the road. They were very happy.

Muffin snored softly in his carriage outside the shop.

They forgot all about him!

Chapter Three

They did not talk much as they walked along. They were too busy eating their candy.

As they turned toward the park, a woman hustled toward them.

"Oh, no!" cried Mary-Anne. "There's Mrs. Belling. She'll want to see the baby."

"Don't worry," replied Josh calmly. "She never has her glasses."

"That's true," agreed Mary-Anne, but something was troubling her.

Then she figured out what it was.

Muffin! The carriage!
We don't have the carriage!
We left it outside the
candy shop!

They both turned and ran back the way they had come. Their boots clattered on the sidewalk.

Outside the shop, the carriage was still there, just as they had left it. They peered inside and saw Muffin still asleep.

As they began to push the carriage again, Mrs. Belling came quickly around the corner.

"My dears!" she said. "How lovely! You're taking the new baby for a walk. What's the little angel's name? What does he weigh? Who does he look like?"

"His name is Muffin," said Josh.

"He hardly weighs anything," said Mary-Anne.

"He looks a lot like his mother," said Josh.

"With pieces of his father," said Mary-Anne.

Mrs. Belling smiled and said, "You funny little things. I'll just peek. I won't wake him."

She leaned forward and looked into the carriage.

She jumped back. She looked again. Then she fumbled in her bag.

She took one last look inside
the carriage. Then she turned and
hurried away up the street without
saying goodbye.

"She didn't seem to mind," said
Mary-Anne. "I hope she doesn't tell
my mother."

They walked on to the park.

27

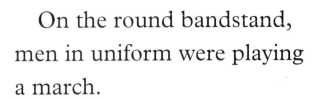

On the round bandstand,
men in uniform were playing
a march.

Mary-Anne and Josh stopped to
listen. They tapped their feet. They
waved their arms. Then they
began marching around. They
couldn't help it.

This time, they did not forget
Muffin. Mary-Anne pushed him
around and around the bandstand
in time to the music.

That baby
will get
seasick!

They were enjoying themselves
so much that they didn't notice that
someone was watching.

A face peered out of the bushes.
It was a dirty face. Mary-Anne and
Josh didn't see the face, but its
eyes certainly saw them.

Chapter Four

Mary-Anne and Josh were out of breath. They sat huffing and puffing on the grass. Then a nanny came along, pushing a very shiny carriage. An older boy walked by her side.

Mary-Anne called to the nanny, "Can you tell me the time, please?"

"Nearly noon," said the nanny.

"Oh, no! Mother will skin me!" yelped Mary-Anne.

The boy peered into the carriage.

Mary-Anne cried, "Never mind him. I have to hurry home."

They pushed the carriage down the path that ran between the trees. They hurried as fast as they could.

Josh looked at the bushes beside the path. He whispered, "Can you hear something?"

Mary-Anne listened. "Yes," she said, "there's something in there."

"It's following us," Josh said in a very quiet voice. "I think it's a big animal. I heard it sniff."

"Wolves!" said Mary-Anne. "They can smell us. They'll hunt us down."

"No, it's human!" yelled Josh. "Run for it!"

They hustled down the path
toward the park gate. But the rustling
and crashing continued. It got faster,
keeping up with them.

Mary-Anne and Josh kept their
hands on the carriage and their eyes
on the gate. Only a little farther …

Then a dark shape shot out of the
bushes and stood in their path.

"Got you," it said.

IT'S
HORRIBLE
HARRY
BANKS!

He was the owner of the dirty
face that had been peering out of
the bushes at them. The rest of him
wasn't too clean, either.

Harry's hair looked even worse than Mary-Anne's. He had better things to do than worry about his hair. On good days, he looked like a hedgehog. On bad days, his hair looked like the brush they used to clean the school toilets.

"Go away, Harry Banks," said
Mary-Anne.

In fact, Mary-Anne kind of liked
Harry. He was more exciting to play
with than Josh was. But she didn't
want Harry to know that.

"Don't have to," said Harry. "It's a
free country. What's in the carriage?"

"It's the baby," said Mary-Anne.
Then she made a silly mistake.

She added, "But you can't look at it."

Now, Harry Banks was not very interested in babies. Until that moment, he had not even wanted to see the baby.

"I can look at it if I want to," he said. "Anyone can look at a baby."

It's not against the law to look at a baby!

"You just can't look at this one," Mary-Anne said very quickly. "This one is different."

"How is it different?" asked Harry, moving closer.

Mary-Anne and Josh stood in front of the carriage.

"We'd like to show him to you, but it might be a shock," said Mary-Anne.

"You might faint," added Josh. "We really should be going now."

Harry stood in the middle of the path, looking puzzled.

"I'll pay you," he said at last.

You can have my best marble.

Mary-Anne and Josh looked at each other. They smiled.

"All right," said Mary-Anne, "but be careful."

Harry handed over his marble. Then, very quietly, he crept up to the carriage.

It's your CAT!

Setting off quickly toward the park gate, Mary-Anne said, "Muffin is a baby."

"Give me my marble back!" Harry yelled, grabbing the carriage handle.

Josh grabbed Harry's sweater. Harry was yelling.

Some kind of rocket shot out of the bushes. It was a barking rocket.

"Get 'em, boy," shouted Harry.

"It's only your mutt, Nip," said Mary-Anne.

Nip danced around, crazy with excitement. He smelled something.

With a leap, Nip was on top of
the carriage.

Muffin woke up because of all
the noise. When he saw Nip, he
exploded out of the shawl and
landed on the path.

Then the kids watched him streak
out of the park gates, still wearing
the bonnet. Behind him raced Nip,
barking happily.

Harry chased after his dog.

Josh was still hanging on to Harry's sweater.

Last of all, Mary-Anne ran along as fast as she could while pushing the carriage. She was really in deep trouble now!

Chapter Five

Mr. Green was arranging the piles of apples in his window.

"My goodness! A cat in a hat! It must be Mary-Anne's kitten," he said as Muffin flew past.

When Josh and Harry hurried by, he said, "What is going on? I must go out and see."

Sorry, Mr. Green.

Muffin ran as fast as he could, but he was only a kitten. He could still hear Nip behind him, panting hard.

In front of Muffin stood a tree. He leapt onto the trunk. He scrambled up with his claws.

Moments later, he sat perched on a high branch, looking down on Nip.

Nip sat under the tree and waited. Harry and Josh arrived next. They were out of breath and mad at each other.

Mary-Anne and the carriage arrived last. She was out of breath, too. She looked up.

Oh, no! Muffin is way up in the tree. We'll never get him down!

"Come to me, Muffin," cooed Mary-Anne. "You'll be safe now."

Muffin stayed where he was.

Mrs. Belling had finished shopping. She was with Mrs. Whiting, and they both saw the children.

"There's something strange about the Burtons' new baby," she whispered to her friend.

"Is there, dear?" her friend replied. "Surely not."

Then Mrs. Belling saw Muffin.

Eek! The baby is up a tree!

Mrs. Whiting tried to calm her. She said, "Don't be silly, dear. It's not a baby. It's a kitten. What happened?"

Mary-Anne explained about Nip, and Mrs. Whiting took charge.

"Harry, Josh, can either of you climb that tree?" she asked.

"Easy, peasy," said Harry, and he started to climb.

As he climbed, Muffin scrambled higher up the tree.

I'm stuck!

"I can't climb any higher," said Harry. His voice sounded more than a bit wobbly.

"Now we've got Harry and Muffin up the tree," sighed Josh.

"Mary-Anne," said Mrs. Whiting. "Run and get Mr. Green. Tell him to bring a stool."

Mr. Green came running. He put the stool under the tree. He climbed up on top and stretched and swayed.

He still couldn't reach either of them.

You could be in the ballet, Mr. Green.

"Wait a minute," said Mrs. Whiting. "The window cleaner does this street on Tuesdays. Run to the corner, Josh, and see if he's coming."

Josh returned with the window cleaner. He was carrying a very long ladder.

For some reason, he also had a very big grin on his face. He set his ladder against the tree.

"Which shall I rescue first?" he asked. "The big creature or the pretty one?"

Mary-Anne began to feel better.

The window cleaner almost ran up the ladder. He didn't mind the height at all. He guided Harry down safely.

"I could have done it if I hadn't gotten stuck," said Harry.

Mary-Anne felt sorry for him and gave him a piece of rock candy.

The window cleaner went up again. This time he stopped under Muffin. Then he made little clicking noises and spoke softly.

He gently put out his hand, and
Muffin let the man pick him up.

He buttoned the kitten into his
jacket and brought him down.

Mary-Anne put Muffin back in
the carriage, and the three children,
followed by Nip, began to walk home.

Chapter Six

It was a sad little parade. Even Nip was quiet. Mary-Anne was worrying about what her mother would say. She still hadn't peeled the potatoes, and it was so late.

Muffin, of course, slept on.

They turned off of Main Street onto the narrow, cobbled lane.

When they reached Mary-Anne's gate, she opened it very quietly.

They crept in one by one, leaving
Nip outside.

The yard was empty. The back
door was still open, but they could
hear no sound inside.

"Mother's gone out to look for
me," gasped Mary-Anne. "Now I'm
in trouble."

"Go and check," said Josh.

Mary-Anne went inside.

Josh took Muffin out of the carriage
and put him to sleep in the sun.

Then he gave the shawl and bonnet
a good shake and pinned them
back on the line.

Mary-Anne
appeared in the
doorway looking
very puzzled.

"They're asleep,"
she whispered. "Even
Mother! She's fast asleep."

"Then get the dinner ready," said Harry. Under his hedgehog hair, he had brains.

Very quietly, they peeled the potatoes and put a pot of water to boil on the stove.

Mary-Anne was not allowed to put coal in the stove, so Harry did it. Soon, they felt the whole kitchen warming up.

They went outside again and stood looking at each other.

"Clean the carriage," said Harry.

Mary-Anne fetched a brush and some rags, and they started to work on the carriage.

Suddenly, above their heads, a window opened.

Mary-Anne?
Is that you?

Mary-Anne's mother was looking out of the window. Then she came hurrying into the yard.

"Oh, dear," she said. "I'm all behind this morning. Baby cried all night, and we both just fell asleep."

Then she realized they were cleaning the carriage.

"Just helping out, Mrs. Burton," said Harry.

"The dinner!" gasped Mother.

"The potatoes are on, Mother," said Mary-Anne. It seemed best not to say anything else.

"Wonderful," said Mrs. Burton. "I'll just heat the stew, and there's some blackberry pie left. You boys must stay and eat. Josh, run and ask your mother. Harry, what about you?"

"Ma won't mind," said Harry. He liked stew and blackberry pie.

They sat around the big wooden table and dug in. Their adventure had made them hungry, but they were on their best behavior.

"Now, what have you been doing today?" Mother asked.

"We went for a little walk," said Mary-Anne. "We saw Mr. Green."

"I hope you remembered your manners," Mrs. Burton said.

"Oh, we did," said Mary-Anne.

"We saw Mrs. Belling, too," she added. "She asked about the baby."

"How kind," Mrs. Burton said. "Did you enjoy yourself, Harry?"

"Well," Harry said, "I guess so."

But he added, "Things are looking up now."

I'm stuck!

"That's excellent," she said, smiling. "So you all had lots to do."

"Not really," said Mary-Anne. "Just the usual."

It was true, you know. That sort of day was usual for Mary-Anne.

Look for More
Read-it!
Chapter Books

The Badcat Gang
Beastly Basil
Cleaner Genie
Clever Monkeys
Contest Crazy
Disgusting Denzil
Duperball
Elvis the Squirrel
Eric's Talking Ears
High Five Hank
Hot Dog and the Talent Competition
Nelly the Monstersitter
On the Ghost Trail
Scratch and Sniff
Sid and Bolter
Stan the Dog Becomes Superdog
The Thing in the Basement
Tough Ronald

Looking for a specific title? A complete list
of *Read-it!* Chapter Books is available on our Web site:
www.picturewindowbooks.com